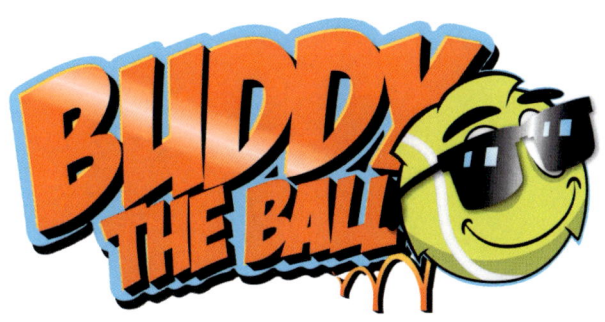

Buddytheball.net

Written and Illustrated by:

Siulyn Christopher

Copyright 2023

Buddy the Ball LLC

All rights reserved.

Bounce Big. Live Bigger.

Hey do you guys want to go outside?

No, thanks, Sushi. We are busy.

It must be here somewhere.

No we are playing
Knight and Princess.

You guys want to play tennis?

Oh man I'm so bored.

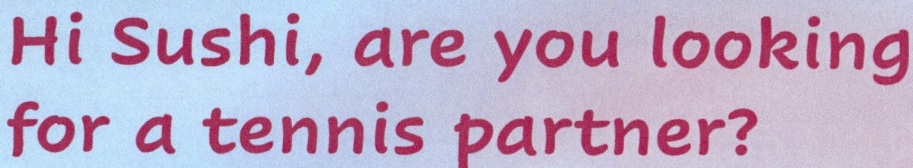

Hi Sushi, are you looking for a tennis partner?

Pow!

Good job!

The next day.

Hi Sushi! Are you ready to kick some more tennis butt!?

I brought Buddy with me.

Hi Sushi!

I won't be able to stay, but Buddy will train you today.

Alright! Are you ready for some real training?

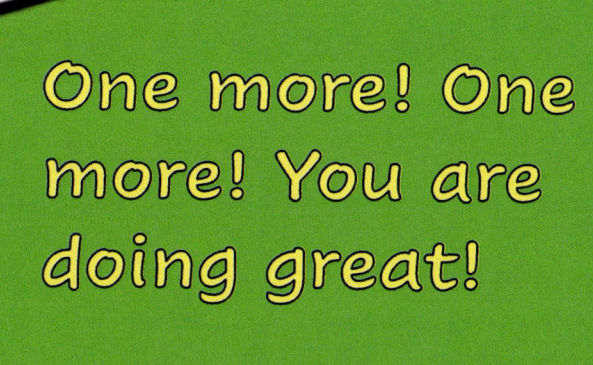
One more! One more! You are doing great!

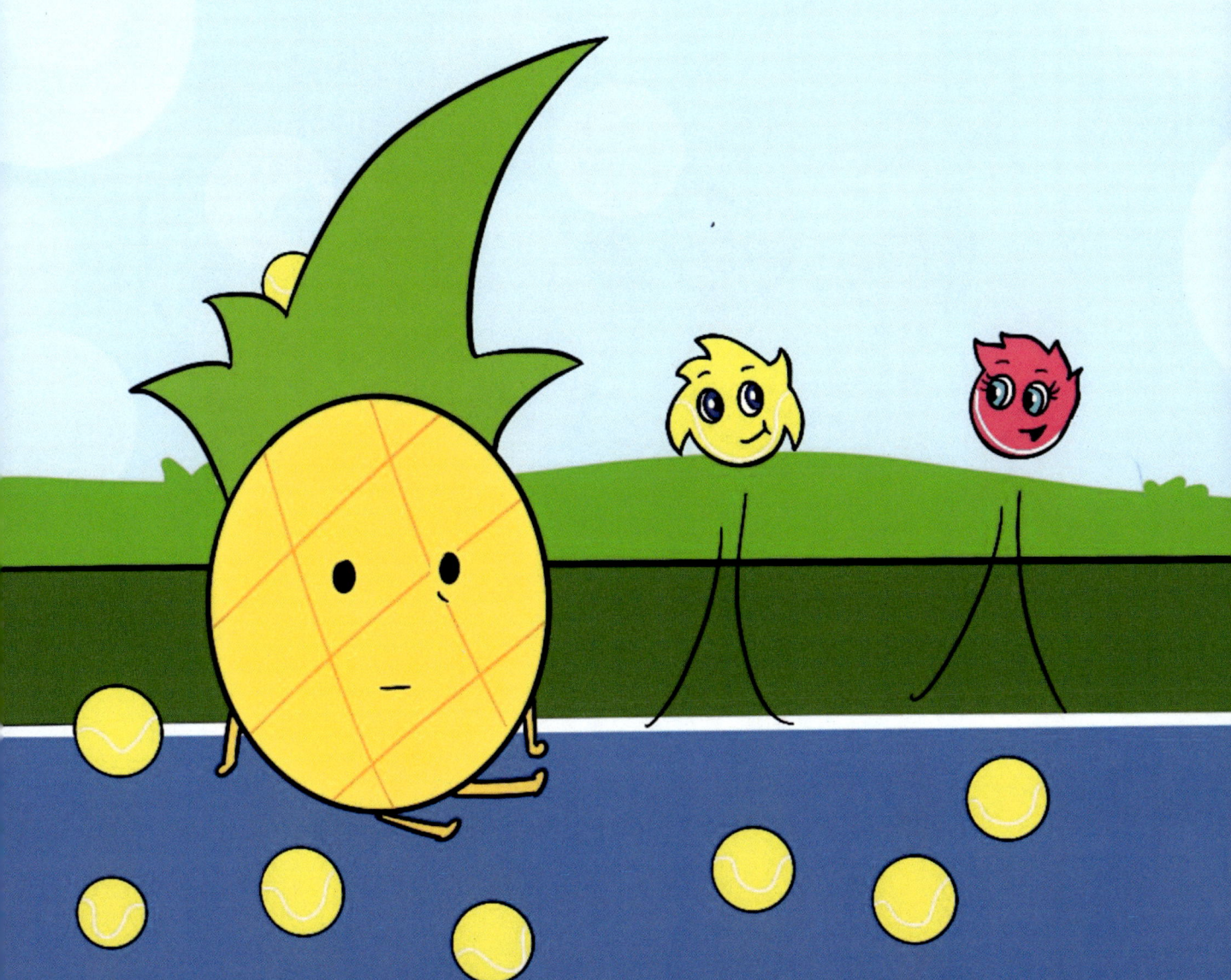

Wow looks like you guys had some great training!

Sushi is really good!

Thanks for helping, Buddy. You are the best!

Muah!

Woa! Who is that?

Buddytheball.net

Made in the USA
Columbia, SC
16 February 2023